W9-AFJ-661

Pictures for Miss Josie

Pictures for Miss Josie

BY

Sandra Belton

PICTURES BY

Benny Andrews

GREENWILLOW BOOKS

An Imprint of HarperCollins*Publishers*

Pictures for Miss Josie

Amistad is an imprint of HarperCollins Publishers, Inc.

Manufactured in China.
www.harperchildrens.com

Collage and oil paints were used to prepare the full-color art.
The text type is 16-point Garamond #3.

Library of Congress Cataloging-in-Publication Data
Belton, Sandra.
Pictures for Miss Josie / by Sandra Belton ; pictures by Benny Andrews.
p. cm.
"Greenwillow Books."

Summary: When his father first takes him to meet Miss Josie, a young boy is somewhat intimidated by her, but through the coming years he comes to treasure her friendship and support and passes on his love of her to his own son. Based on the life of Josephine Carroll Smith.
ISBN 0-688-17480-9 (trade). ISBN 0-688-17481-7 (lib. bdg.)
1. African Americans—Juvenile fiction. [1. African Americans—Fiction. 2. Self-esteem—Fiction.] I. Andrews, Benny, (date) ill. II. Title.
PZ7.B4797 Pi 2003 [E]—dc21 2002006797

10 9 8 7 6 5 4 3 2 1 First Edition

Greenwillow Books

For William Waller Thompson,
Aunt Jo's best,
and always for
Allen Douglass
—S. B.

To my mother,
Mrs. Viola P. Andrews
—B. A.

It was the beginning of the proud times when he saw her first. She was like a giant, standing there in front of the sun. Against the row of houses without yards in between.

He wondered if she was the one who had pushed all the houses together.

"Come over here, young man, and give me a hug!" she said. The voice was strong and big. The arms, too. They held him tight.

"You're going to squeeze the life out of him, Josie," the man said. Her husband.

The arms got tighter. "I've been waiting a long time to have this baby in my arms," she said.

He wondered if she would give him some of the peppermint he could smell on her cheek.

The day had already been packed with firsts. A first trip with Dad. A first train ride. A first finding out of something amazing about Dad.

"Yes, son, I worked on the trains when I was a young man. I waited on tables in the dining car."

And now a first meeting of Miss Josie, at last.

"She's one of the finest persons I know," Dad had said again and again. "When I was a poor student, she welcomed me into her home and treated me like family. Without Miss Josie I might never have made it through school."

And another big first was still to come. His dad would be leaving him behind with Miss Josie. For the rest of the day and all of the night. It was a first he wasn't sure he wanted.

TO T
210

"You'll be fine," his dad said.

"Of course he will," Miss Josie's strong, big voice said. "He'll be better than fine."

He wondered if he could scream, "No, I won't!" and if he was too big to cry.

The inside of the pushed-together house was crowded with pictures. More pictures than he had ever seen in one place.

"This is me when I was about your age," Miss Josie said. "This picture was taken in Georgetown where I grew up."

He wondered what it would be like to make so many pictures. It made him smile for the first time.

"You like pictures?" she asked, as if she knew.

His head went up and down, saying "Yes."

"You like to make pictures?" she asked again.

His head went up and down again. Faster than before. And when he smiled this time, his teeth showed through.

She smiled, too. "Then that's what you'll do right now," she said. "Make pictures."

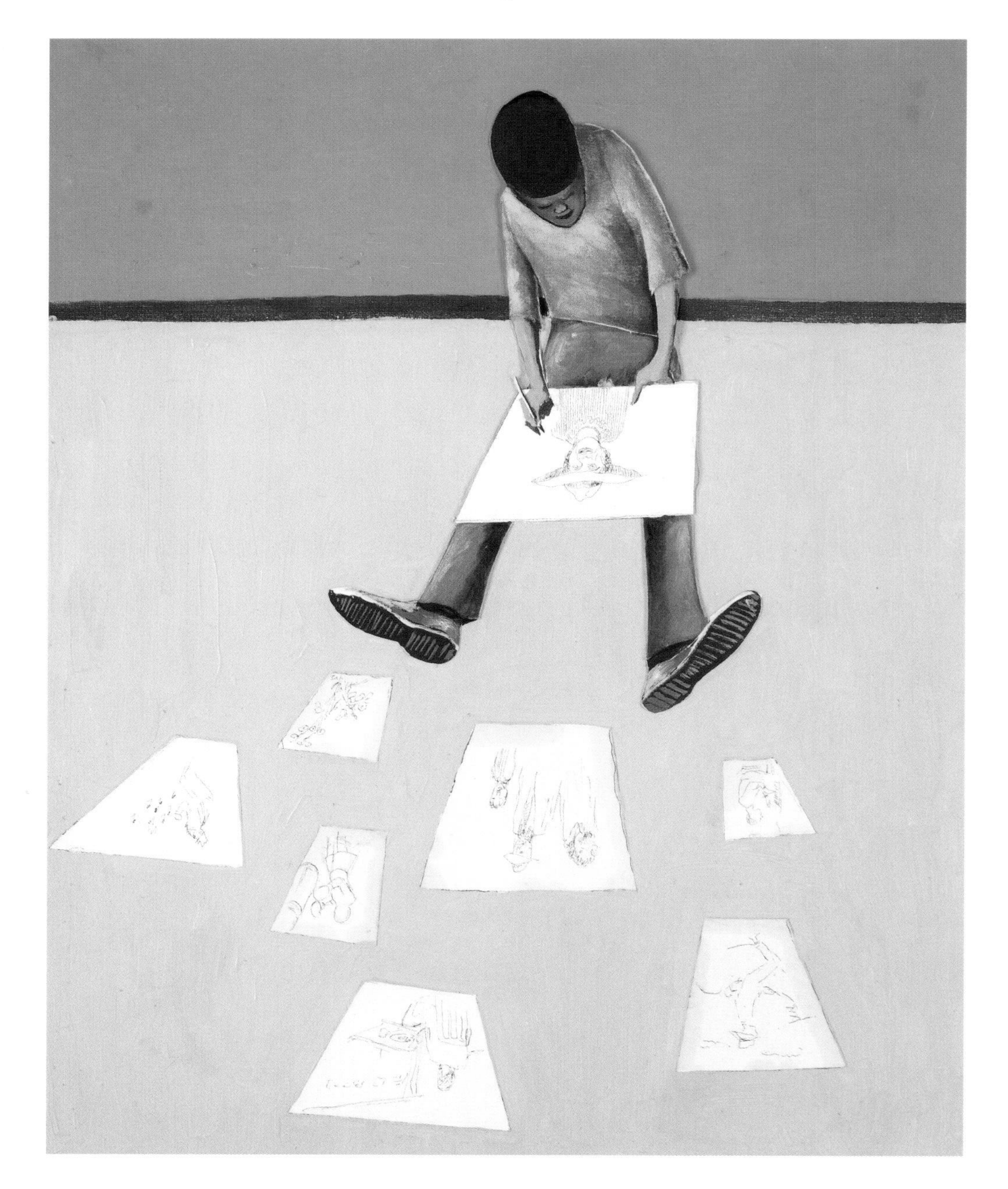

That's what he did. All the rest of that day and into the night. All while Miss Josie and her husband listened to the radio. Sometimes they hummed along and patted their feet. Once they even danced along and laughed at themselves.

He stopped wondering when his dad would be coming to pick him up.

The next day he went for a walk with Miss Josie. She showed him things he had never even imagined before. Buildings with round tops and monuments like towers. People dancing on grass without buildings in the way.

They ate sweet purple ice and listened to the music.

"Maybe you'll put some of these things in your pictures," she said. "Then others can enjoy them, too."

He wondered if he would remember everything to tell his friends back home.

A few years passed before he saw her next. Years during which he became a reflection of his father. Years during which she became the head of a school in the capital city. Proud times for all of them.

Soon he would be taking his first train ride by himself.

"Miss Josie will meet you at Union Station," his father said. "She'll stay with you while you wait for the next train you have to catch. She'll probably take you to lunch."

He wondered if he'd be able to order anything he wanted from the menu.

His father said to wait for Miss Josie inside the station. In the enormous room whose ceiling rose to the sky.

"Keep an eye out for her," his father said. "You'll probably see her before she sees you."

TRAINS

He sat on one of the benches and watched the doors while he waited. Then it was just the way his father had said. His eye caught Miss Josie coming before she could see him at all.

She was still like a giant, standing there in front of the sun. Looking stern and foreboding. Like she could push the waiting-room benches together without any trouble.

He knew a lot more than he had all those years before. She was just a woman. And a fine person at that.

But knowing didn't keep her from looking scary. Or keep him from sliding down in his seat and holding his tablet for drawing in front of his face.

He sat very still and watched her walking. Circling that waiting room three times in all. Looking everywhere for him while she circled. Looking and looking but never finding.

He wondered what she would have said to him if she had ever seen him that day.

CAMP NEWS
BULLETIN BOARD

He called home that night to say he was at camp and safe.

"I was worried, son," his father said. "Miss Josie said you weren't in the station."

"I was there," he said to his father. "I guess Miss Josie just didn't see me."

He wondered if he would ever tell the whole truth about that day in Union Station.

When he saw Miss Josie next, she was a leader for all of the schools in her city. He was in college in the same city. His first year.

"Miss Josie wants you to visit her whenever you can," his father had told him. "It'll be like having a home away from home."

He didn't want to be anywhere but at college. What a place it was to be! More fun than he could have ever imagined. Always something new to see and do.

Miss Josie called one Sunday morning. Asked him to go with her to church and then to come for dinner.

He wondered if he should tell her he'd make it another time. But finally he decided to go. To get the visit over with. And make his father happy.

She was standing there in front of the sun. At the door of Shiloh, her most-loved church. When he came beside her, he had to bend to give a kiss that said "Hello." He caught the smell of peppermint on her cheek.

He wondered for the first time why she had ever seemed like a giant too scary to be near.

The inside of her church burst with words and music. Miss Josie rocked and sang. Her voice was loud and her singing off-key. It made him smile and want to sing along.

After the sermon she took him around, telling everybody who he was. "He's the son of one of my boys. Now he's my boy, too."

He wondered if coming here for church every Sunday morning might be a good thing to do.

Dinner that day turned into a new beginning. For laughing and talking and having a good time with Miss Josie, whose husband had passed on. For breaking bread at her delicious table. For finding a home away from home. Just the way his dad had said.

He decided to stop the old wondering. All he had heard about Miss Josie was true.

Their proud times got better as those college years went by. He'd found a friend for talking to. She'd found a new son for helping.

"Dad says I shouldn't waste so much time on my pictures," he said. "He wants me to learn things that'll help me get a job."

Her look was stern but her voice softer than usual. Making sure he would listen well.

"Your father loves you and wants the best for you," she said. "But you have a gift and a dream. It's up to you to put them to good use."

Then came the day he was like a giant, standing there in front of the sun. Receiving a piece of proof for his hard work well done.

Miss Josie was there with his parents. Clapping and cheering. Happy in her soul to see the time come. Not wondering at all how it had come to be.

A few years passed before the next celebration. Miss Josie came on that day, too.

He saw her changed in many ways. Moving slower. Talking louder and hearing less. Very little at all.

But in all the ways that mattered, she was still the same.

The joy of celebration lasted into the night. Something for everyone to remember for a long, long time.

More years passed. His family grew, just as his father's had. Now he had a son of his own.

He passed on the stories that had been passed on to him. About Miss Josie. About the things he wanted his son to know and himself to remember.

"She's one of the finest persons I know," he said over and over. "If it hadn't been for Miss Josie, I might have given up trying to be what I am."

Then it was time for his son's proud times to get started. A first plane trip and subway ride. A first walk with Dad through the streets of the capital city. Another first meeting of Miss Josie, at last.

It was one of the proudest times ever. Seeing his own son wrapped by Miss Josie. A very different Miss Josie. But in the ways that mattered, still the same.

"My hearing's just about gone," she said. Her voice louder than ever. "Just about gone."

His head went up and down, saying "Yes." And when he smiled at Miss Josie, his teeth showed through.

The words of his gift spoke loud in their silence. They were heard all over the room. "We've had some proud times, Miss Josie. Indeed we have."

And they were there. All of them. The proud times he had brought for Miss Josie to remember.

That day was one of the very, very best. One they were all sorry to see come to an end.

"Bye, Miss Josie," his son said. Moving his mouth slow to make every word clear. "I love you."

Miss Josie waved and threw a kiss. A giant of a woman, standing there in the sun.

Josephine Carroll Smith (1894–1997)

This story is written to honor the memory of Josephine Carroll Smith, a much-loved "Miss Josie."

Mrs. Smith was born and lived her entire life in Washington, D.C. She was the only sister of seven brothers, all born to parents who had been enslaved and made certain their children had a knowledge of what it was like *not* to be free. These parents passed on to their children a very great treasure: a belief in themselves and all they could become.

During her lifetime Josephine Carroll Smith became a teacher and later a principal. By the time she retired from the school system of the District of Columbia, she had become the Director of Elementary Education in charge of administration. In this role she was responsible for drawing up the boundaries for the desegregation of all of the schools in Washington, D.C.—boundaries showing which schools all children would attend, black and white alike.

Mrs. Smith bore no children. However, over the years she opened her home, her heart, and her purse to numerous young black men who were struggling to educate themselves. They became her sons. Because of her generous support and encouragement, each of them succeeded. Their families came to know, respect, and love dear "Aunt Jo" as they did.

Josephine Carroll Smith lived to be 103 years of age. It was a long and success-filled life; she is greatly missed. Those who knew her might take some comfort in the West African folktale that teaches:

People are alive as long as we remember them.

So let it be.

—*Sandra Belton*